Getting to Omaha and the NCAA Men's College World Series

Copyright © 2012 by Valerie Doherty

All rights reserved. No part of this publication may be reproduced or transmitted in any form or by any means, electronic or mechanical, including photocopy, recording, or any information storage and retrieval system, without permission in writing from the publisher.

NCAA, College World Series and CWS are registered trademarks of the National Collegiate Athletic Association.

Requests for permission to make copies of any part of the work should be submitted online at info@mascotbooks.com or mailed to Mascot Books, 560 Herndon Parkway #120, Herndon, VA 20170.

PRT0612A

Printed in the United States

ISBN-13: 9781937406325
ISBN-10: 1937406326

www.mascotbooks.com

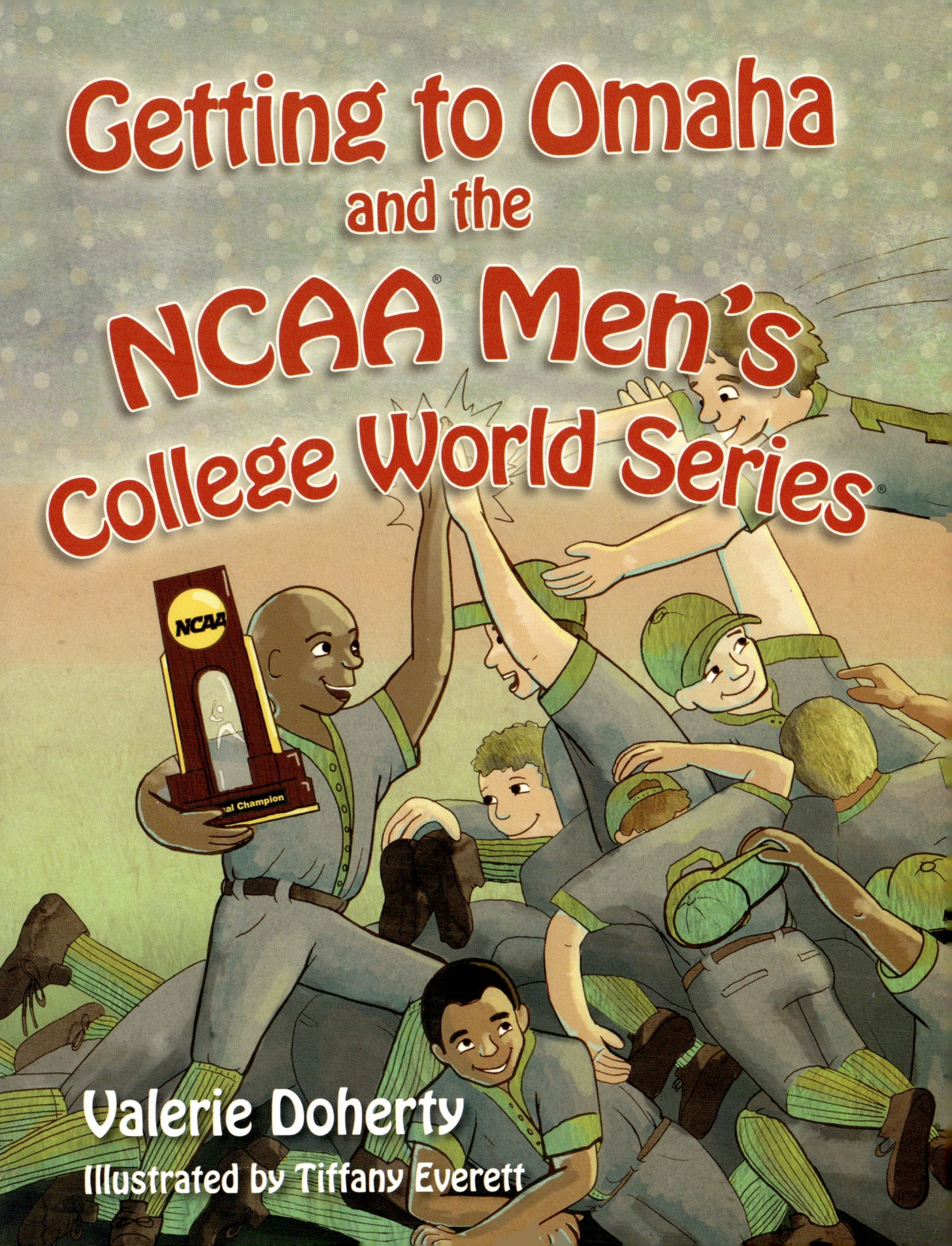

When Old Man Winter says goodbye for another year, the boys of the diamond dream of getting to Omaha and the NCAA Men's College World Series. The history and heart of college baseball keeps on beating in the middle of the Great Plains. The game has been played in the midwest city for as long as many can remember.

For two weeks in June, players, coaches, and fans welcome summer with the sights and sounds of this college baseball celebration. For the teams that have made the trip before, the goal is to "Get back to Omaha." For those who have yet to make the journey, the new season means another chance.

Every team dreams of being in a championship dogpile and bringing a NCAA Men's College World Series trophy home. Spring practice begins with promise and purpose. Days are filled with stretching, hitting, pitching, and fielding. When the first game finally arrives, there is joy in the ump's excited shout,

"Play ball!"

There are team traditions, lucky mascots, and rally caps to guide a team to victory.
And always, there are the fans that hope and cheer, "Maybe this is the year we get to Omaha."
Conference champs are crowned. Regionals and super regionals are waiting to be won. With every pitch and run, Omaha gets closer.

There are nail biters and close calls. There are no-hitters and grand slams. In every team's heart, they hear a voice saying, "This is our year. We're going to the NCAA Men's College World Series."

Players, young and old, talk about their first look at the diamond when they get to the Series. Some remember the green outfield. Some remember the pitcher's mound. Some touch the dirt to make certain they have really arrived.

"Can't believe it's true.
We're glad to be here, Omaha!"

There are memories of games played at an old park-Rosenblatt: the Diamond on the Hill. Close your eyes and see it all: the neighborhood, the tents, the colors, the field, and always, the teams. The Series has a new home now, with bright beginnings and fresh stories to be told.

For the hometown fans, the Series is a wonderful time. There are returning friends and new visitors to greet. There are opening ceremonies, parades, good-time barbecues, and fireworks in a summer sky.
With bats and gloves in hand, children wait for players' autographs. There are hellos and smiles all around. No one is a stranger for long.

The first game of a championship series begins. There are high hopes for the lucky eight teams.
Players and Presidents throw the first pitch. "Play ball!" There is joy in these June days!

Families celebrate Father's Day. Sons, fathers, and grandchildren love the games even more because they are together.

There are cheers for the underdogs and chants for the favorites. There are seventh-inning stretches and songs to be sung.
There are hot dogs and popcorn. How about some peanuts to share? Take me out to the old ball game! There's not a better place to be!

The teams play on in sun, rain, and heat. "We've made it to Omaha. We want to WIN it now!"
Championship Game! "We've said goodbye to the others. Maybe next year they'll be back. Tonight is THIS team's time to shine."
There are many NCAA Men's College World Series baseball teams. They travel from many cities and states. They wear different team colors. Some are long shots. Some are back-to-back champs. Everyone loves the game. It's in their step as the players run on the field.

There are downtown hits, big rallies, and bottom of the ninth homers to decide championships. There are victory dogpiles, team photos, and "tough win" trophies to take home. Some players travel to the big league after the Series. Some play their last college game. For others, they wait anxiously for spring and the hope of a new season.

Teams are ready. When Old Man Winter says goodbye for another year, the boys of the diamond dream of getting to Omaha and the NCAA Men's College World Series.

The End

About the Author:

Valerie Doherty is a graduate of the University of Nebraska - Lincoln and University of Illinois. As a college baseball fan, she has enjoyed many exciting games at the NCAA Men's College World Series. *Getting to Omaha...* honors this yearly event. This is her second publication with Mascot Books.